DR DEATH

Powerless Earth - Novelette One

Paul McMurrough

British Library Cataloguing-in-Publication Data

A catalogue record for this book is available from the British Library

First paperback edition June 2022

ISBN: 9781838066079

..

FOREWORD

This story is based on characters from the book Reliance, book one of the Powerless Earth series. It is set one day after the end of Reliance.

For continuity and your enjoyment, I would suggest that you read Reliance before reading this story.

Dyslexia Friendly

As someone who has struggled with dyslexia all my life, it was important to me to release a version of this book in a Dyslexia Friendly format. I understand that dyslexia affects people differently and so the changes to presentation and formatting that I have made may not help everyone, but I do hope that you find it easier and more comfortable to read.

Dr Death contains some strong language and themes of violence, and therefore may not be suitable for a younger audience.

CHAPTER 1

George propped the heavy shotgun against the wall beside his wife's bed and leaned over to place a kiss on her forehead. He grimaced and groaned as a bolt of pain from his ribs seared through him. Carefully, he adjusted the patchwork quilt, tucking it neatly around her frail body.

Easing himself painfully onto the stool, he rested his elbows on the bed and cradled his head. Exhausted from the trauma of the day before and from standing guard all night, he so wanted to lie down beside his Rose and let sleep take him.

He looked at the many bottles of pills sitting on the bedside table, most of them nearly empty. Behind them sat a photo from one of their holidays during better times. They stood arm in arm on some dock in front of a huge cruise ship. He couldn't remember exactly where it was, a stopover somewhere during their last Mediterranean cruise. *Rose would remember*, he thought. She was always the one who did the planning, and could recall every detail when they returned home. She loved to travel, to explore new places and meet new people. George was just happy to follow. He didn't really care where they were as long as they were together.

He lifted the silver-framed photo and used the edge of the quilt to clear a little speck of dust from Rose's cheek. The joy on their faces made him smile. They looked so happy — Rose in a beautiful summer dress and a wide-brimmed white sun hat, him in a garishly colourful Hawaiian shirt — one of many that Rose had bought him over the years for their trips. Her smile could light up a room. He longed for those days again. They hadn't been blessed with children and so had taken every opportunity to travel, right up until the previous summer, just before Rose had taken ill. George's smile faded, and a tear collected at the corner of his eye. He knew there would be no more trips.

"Where was this?" he said to no one.

"Barcelona 2012," came the reply in a soft, whispered voice.

George looked up, surprised that Rose was awake, but more so that she was able to remember. She'd barely been conscious at all over the past few days and when she had; she'd been confused and incoherent. She'd even slept through the gunshots the day before.

George's face lit up. "Good morning, my love."

"That was our Mediterranean cruise," said Rose with a weak smile. "How do you not remember that?"

"I didn't care where it was, love. I was just following you," said George with a chuckle.

"What happened to your head, George?" asked Rose, seeing the wound on his head which he'd half-heartedly bandaged.

"Ah, it's nothing. I just bumped my head."

"It looks like it's still bleeding. You might need stitches." Rose tried in vain to push herself up onto her pillow.

"Here, let me help you, love," said George as he lifted her head and adjusted her pillows. "Can I get you something?"

"Just some water, please, love."

George held up a plastic cup of water and positioned the straw. Rose took a sip and wet her dry lips.

"That was Barcelona, do you not remember? We asked a young lad to take our photo, and you thought he was going to steal our camera cause he kept backing away to get a better angle," said Rose with a chuckle. "You kept shuffling forward every time he moved back."

George laughed. "Yeah, well, you can never be sure."

"That was the same year you sang New York, New York at the karaoke night," she said, her shoulders shaking as she laughed and struggled for a breath, "and they stopped the music before the end cause you were so bad."

George hid behind his hand and shook his head. "You forced me to get up, and you knew I couldn't sing," he said, joining her laughter.

"We're never doing that again," he said with a laugh, the words coming before he could stop them. *Of course they wouldn't.*

Rose smiled in acceptance and regret.

George couldn't believe how alert and alive his wife seemed. He hadn't seen her laugh in so long. She was thin and frail, but when she laughed, he could see the cheeky, fun-loving woman who he'd shared the last sixty years with. He didn't want the moment to end.

"Go and get the big photo album," said Rose, still beaming. "I think there's a photo of you on stage in it."

George gave an exaggerated frown, but there was nothing else he'd rather do, and so he rose stiffly and went to fetch their leather-bound book of memories.

With his pains and tiredness forgotten, George sat beside his wife and flicked through the photos of their many trips — pausing at each photo to reminisce. He spent more time looking at the joy on his wife's face than at the actual photos. She was everything to him. Without her, he'd have no place in this new cold and dark world.

CHAPTER 2

Doctor Brian Angelo adjusted his tie in the small circular mirror above the sink. His only collared shirt was a now baggy and loose around his neck. He'd spent the previous hour spit-polishing his dress shoes with the corner of a towel, more to pass the time than anything else. It'd been nearly ten years since he'd last dressed so formally. His normal attire of sweatshirt, sweatpants, and trainers were now neatly folded and placed on the edge of his bed. He was thankful that prisoners in Northern Ireland were allowed to wear their own clothes. He wouldn't want to be leaving in an orange jumpsuit or something with the establishment's name stencilled on the back. After one last look in the mirror, he approached the door and craned his neck to look up and down the corridor.

With the recreation area surprisingly quiet, he took a cautious step out of his cell. Most of the prisoners had already left, either the day before or throughout the night, gradually filtering out in small groups or alone. The paramilitary prisoners, who'd been left with the keys to the inner sections of the prison when the guards had withdrawn, eventually gained access to the outer doors and bolted for freedom as soon as they'd forced them open.

Most of the other prisoners, including Brian, had stayed in their cells or in the canteen where multiple fights had broken out over what remained of the food and fresh water. They believed what they'd been told by Supervisor Henderson, that the army would be arriving at any time to take control. It was now the third day since Derek Henderson and the rest of the

guards had abandoned them, and still no one
had come.

Brian liked to think Derek really did believe
that the army would come, and that he hadn't
just sealed them all inside to starve to death.
But what'd he think was going to happen when
the prisoners had been let out of their cells to
roam free?

What did happen was anarchy. Rather than
take any kind of control or responsibility, the
paramilitary prisoners had rallied around their
respective leaders and immediately set out to
find a way through the outer doors to their
freedom. *At least they'd the decency to open
the individual cells first*, thought Brian.

Most of the other prisoners, driven by thirst
and hunger, made their way to the canteen in
search of the remaining supplies. What ensued
was a frenzied and barbaric scene as inmates
clambered over one another to secure a share
of the food and water. Control of the canteen

changed hands repeatedly during the first day, as temporary alliances were forged and broken. Of course, Brian didn't get involved. He didn't have the temperament or physique for such violence. Instead, he remained in the relative safety of his cell.

It was common knowledge that Brian had been a doctor on the outside, and so many of the injured came, or were brought, to him for help. Injuries ranged from broken bones and suspected concussions, to cuts and stab wounds. With no instruments and very little medical supplies, he could provide nothing but the most basic of care. But even this level of usefulness afforded him some measure of protection from the roaming gangs of thugs who looked to take their anger and frustration out on someone. He'd heard rumours of savage beatings being dished out to some of the less desirable residents — the sex offenders and paedophiles, who'd cowered together in a couple of cells for safety. None of them had been brought to him for treatment, which was either a very good sign or a very bad sign.

Two of Brian's neighbours stood by the pool table, arguing over their next move.

"Come on, we need to get out of here," said Thomas Campbell as he shifted from foot to foot in an agitated jig. A career petty thief in his early thirties, Thomas was about halfway through his latest five-year stretch. "No one is coming."

"I'm not going anywhere," said Dermot Moore as he perched on the edge of the pool table, legs dangling and arms folded defiantly across his chest. "I've less than two weeks left. I'm not going to mess that up now by doing a bunk."

"So what're you gonna do, stay here and fuckin' starve to death?"

"They said the army would come. I'm just gonna wait."

"Look," said Thomas, pointing at Brian, "even Dr Death is leggin' it."

Brian was aware of the nickname that his fellow inmates had given him — actually, it'd been the tabloid newspapers who'd come up with the label when they reported on his conviction, among others like Angel of Death, which he thought was clever, and The Euthanizer, which had a kind of superhero ring to it, he liked that too. They'd sentenced him to twenty years for the murder of six of his elderly patients. *If they only knew the real number*, he thought.

"Tell him, Doc," said Thomas. "Nobody's coming. We need to get out of here."

Brian shrugged. "Certainly looks that way."

"But when the power comes back on, they'll round us all up, won't they, Doc?" asked Dermot. "They'll double our sentences for escaping, won't they?"

"Well, they'll certainly round us up anyway, but I doubt they'll be too harsh," said Brian. "As long as you haven't been involved in those riots in the canteen or the beatings. Just make sure you behave yourselves if you do leave."

"But I've only two weeks left," said Dermot, desperate for someone smarter than him, of which there were many, to tell him what to do.

"You'll not fuckin' make it two weeks in here with no food, you muppet," said Thomas with a snort.

Dermot looked at his friend, then back to Brian, the enormity of his dilemma seeming to paralyse him.

"Where're you heading to, Doc?" asked Dermot.

"Not sure yet, but I can't stay here any longer without food."

"Can I come with you?" Dermot asked, suddenly seeming like a lost child.

Brian felt for him, but taking him with him was not an option — he had work to do. People out there needed his help.

"That wouldn't be a good idea, Thomas. You two would be better sticking together," said Brian.

"Look like you're going for a job interview, Doc," said Thomas, nudging his mate and laughing. "Hope it's not in an old people's home."

Brian's mouth curled into a smile — his eyes did not. "Good luck, boys," he said as he turned and headed for the door, leaving the two inmates, who were now in hysterics, to finish their debate.

He made his way through the unfamiliar corridors, areas of the prison that were normally off limits to inmates, and finally came upon the outer door which had been pried off its hinges. Stepping out into the staff carpark, Brian paused and looked up at the turbulent grey sky. He closed his eyes and savoured the crisp, clean air.

CHAPTER 3

The whistle of the boiling kettle on the gas stove jolted George from a half doze as he rested heavily against the kitchen counter. He was tired and sore, but he hadn't felt as happy in a long time — which was ironic given the fact that his kitchen looked like a fight scene from an old western. Broken furniture lay all around, the busted back door was wedged closed with the only remaining kitchen chair, and a pool of drying blood stained the floor — straight fingers of the black-red liquid stretched out along the joints between the tiles, marking the spot where George had killed a man less than twenty-four hours before.

Filling the two cups, which he'd arranged on the floral-patterned plastic tray, he considered his options for carrying both the tray and the huge shotgun up the stairs at the same time. The grip in his ageing hands wasn't what it used to be, and the stairs were a challenge at the best of times, but after some careful balancing and adjustment he managed to find an arrangement that would work.

"Here we go," said George as he manoeuvred his way into his wife's bedroom. "A nice cup of tea for my beautiful bride..." the words trailed off as he realised that Rose had drifted off to sleep again. He placed the tray on the bedside table, nudging the medication to the side, and fussed at the quilt again before risking another stab of pain to place a kiss on Rose's forehead. She shifted slightly but didn't wake.

George smiled and let out a long sigh as he gazed down at his wife. He chuckled at the absurdly colourful Hawaiian shirt he'd put on to surprise her. She'd have loved it. *She'll see it later*, he thought. He just hoped that she'd still be in such great form. Lifting his mug of tea and the increasingly weighty shotgun, he shuffled out. He'd get some fresh flowers from the garden for when she woke again.

George leaned against the splintered door frame and looked out across his front garden and the fields beyond. Lisa's bright yellow car was still wedged against his gatepost, the bonnet folded upwards like a kid's tent and a spider's web of cracks stretched across the windscreen. Apart from that — and the three dead bodies grotesquely displayed on his lawn — the scene looked like any other day.

He took a sip from his mug of tea and stared at the three men who'd invaded his home. Two of them had died at his hands, but he felt no remorse. He did feel a little uncomfortable with the fact that they'd been dumped in a heap, but there was a reason for that; they were a deterrent to any other escaped prisoners who may have a mind to pay him a visit. *Beware the crazy old man with a shotgun*, he thought.

The sky was dark and heavy with approaching rain. George squinted over his mug to focus on a hobbling figure in the distance. *Another of Her Majesty's residents out for a stroll*, he thought, as he lifted the shotgun and balanced it casually over his forearm, making sure to conceal the effort that it took. He sipped on his cooling tea as the figure slowly grew bigger. He was glad he'd put his cardigan over the Hawaiian shirt. He wanted to look menacing, but not completely insane. The stranger would likely keep going, but George would watch to make sure that he did.

As the figure approached, George was surprised to make out a middle-aged man, well dressed in a shirt and tie, and an ill-fitting suit jacket. He was struggling, and every other step came with a painful looking limp.

George stooped to set his mug on the doorstep and raised the shotgun slightly as the man nodded an acknowledgement.

Getting no response from George, the man stopped beside the crashed car and spoke in a hoarse, laboured voice, "That looks nasty. Was someone hurt?"

George didn't respond, other than to make a show of raising the shotgun further when the man approached the gate.

"I don't want any trouble, sir," said the man, raising his hands slightly. His focus immediately going to the three dead bodies.

"Unless you want to join them, you'll move on," said George, tilting the barrel of the large shotgun a couple of degrees higher.

"Honestly, sir, I'm no threat."

"So you haven't just escaped from the prison?" said George with an exaggerated rise of his eyebrows.

"Oh no, I am from the prison, but I wouldn't say I escaped," said the man. "The doors were open and there's no food left, so most of the people have just left."

"When *people*, and I think you mean prisoners, just leave, I think that's called escaping," said George, feeling like he'd already engaged with this latest visitor for too long.

"We were left with no option. The guards abandoned us days ago. I'm sure most of us will surrender ourselves once everything is back to normal."

"Well, these three won't," said George flatly.

The man continued to stare at the bodies. "No, I suppose not. What happened? Is someone else hurt?"

"They attacked me in my home. I killed them," said George with uncharacteristic coldness. "Okay, enough chat, move on." He gestured to the road with the shotgun.

"That looks like a nasty cut on your head."

"Don't worry about it. On you go," said George more forcefully, raising the gun and pointing it straight at the escaped prisoner.

"I used to be a doctor — I could dress it properly for you," said the man, raising his hands defensively again.

"Is that right? So why are you in prison?"

"A disagreement with the tax man," said the man sheepishly.

George studied him — well-spoken, ageing and frail — he certainly didn't look like a criminal, and certainly not a violent one. He'd all but given up on getting medical help for his wife. *But what were the chances of a real doctor just strolling past*? he thought.

"Look, I understand. You've no reason to believe a word I say. I'm sorry for disturbing you. I'll be on my way, but would you have a little food or water to spare? I've barely eaten in three days."

George lowered the gun slightly but didn't respond.

"Okay sir, I get it. I'll be on my way," said the man as he slowly turned to continue his journey.

"Wait," said George with a sigh. "Stay where you are and I'll get you something, but if you take a step closer I'll blow your fuckin' head off, do you understand?"

"Absolutely, thank you so much."

CHAPTER 4

Brian watched as the elderly man retreated inside and closed the door. He stared down at the three bodies lying side by side on the unkempt front garden. They'd been dumped without care rather than placed with reverence.

He knew these men. It'd been one of them that'd unlocked the cells in his wing. The closest body lay face up. It was obvious from the gapping wound in his chest that this elderly resident knew how to use the huge shotgun.

Brian gazed down at the bodies with curiosity — he hadn't seen a dead body in so long. He missed it, the peace and purity. But there was an emptiness — he'd missed the exciting part — the moment of the last breath when the soul was released and sent on its journey to a better place. He missed the responsibility, the righteous duty, the power. He yearned for that rush again.

The creaking of the door shook Brian from his musing. The elderly man appeared again at the door with a plastic cup in one hand and a large red apple in the other — the shotgun wedged under his armpit and balancing across his left forearm.

"I told you not to come any closer."

"I'm sorry, I was just curious," said Brian, backing away.

"Humm, go back to the gate and I'll put these down for you."

Brian retreated to the gate and watched as the elderly man took a couple of unsteady steps towards him and placed the cup and the apple on a small wall that bordered the driveway.

"Thank you so much, sir," said Brian.

The elderly man grunted an acknowledgement and retraced his steps to the front door.

"I'm Dr Brian Thompson," said Brian. He thought is wise to give a false surname just in case Angelo stirred a memory.

"George," said the elderly man with a nod.

"It's nice to meet you, George. You don't know what this means to me. Thank you," said Brian, the last of his words lost in the plastic cup as he drained most of the water.

"What kind of doctor were you?" asked George, angling the heavy-looking gun so it no longer pointed directly at Brian.

"I was a GP for twenty years, and then I specialised in geriatric care," said Brian over a mouthful of apple. He wiped the dripping juice from his lips with his sleeve and smiled, "I'm sorry George, I'm just so hungry."

Brian registered George's sudden change in demeanour. Had he remembered him from an old news report? Brian tensed, expecting the shotgun to be levelled at him again. But instead George lowered the gun further.

"Listen, that cut on your head is obviously still bleeding George, you should really let me look at it," said Brian, nodding to George's forehead before taking another large bite of the apple. A widening spot of fresh blood was visible through George's makeshift bandage.

"How do I know I can trust you?"

"I assure you I'm not a violent man, George. Yes, I broke the law and now I'm paying for it," said Brian, lowering his head in false shame.

George bobbed his head, but he still appeared sceptical.

"It's a lame excuse I know, but I trusted a crooked accountant with my finances and ..."

George cut across him, "My wife is upstairs, she's very poorly and I can't get through to the hospital or her doctor." The defiance in

George's voice had given way to hope, or maybe desperation.

Oh, now isn't that twist of fate, thought Brian.

"It's lucky that I came this way now, isn't?" said Brian as he took a tentative step forward. "Please let me see if I can help. I promise I'm not a threat to you. I've taken an oath to do no harm after all, and regardless of the fact that I'm a prisoner, that oath still stands."

"Okay," said George.

Brian smiled and took another step towards George.

"We'll get that head sorted first, then I can have a look at your wife," said Brian.

"But I'm telling you, one step out of line and you'll join your mates here, and believe me, I'll not lose a minute's sleep over it. You understand?"

"I do George. I completely understand, and I don't blame you for being cautious."

George stepped to the side and gestured for Brian to enter before directing him to the kitchen.

"Careful where you step," said George as they traversed the dark hallway.

Brian stayed close to the wall to avoid the obvious hazard, a large pool of blood about halfway along the hall and a continuous streak all the way to the front door, left presumably when George had dragged the bodies out. *He must be stronger than he looks*, thought Brian.

CHAPTER 5

George followed the doctor into the kitchen. With the sky darkening, the light from the window above the sink did little to cut through the gloom. The room seemed smaller in the poor light. *What am I doing*? He thought, questioning his decision to let this escaped convict into his house. He knew the shotgun was of little use at close quarters, but he didn't want to just set it down and let this guy bandage him up.

"You can take that chair from the door and have a seat," said George.

"No, no, I'll need you to sit down so that I can look at that cut," said Brian.

"I will in a minute, but you just have a seat in the meantime, okay?" said George, making it clear that he was still in control.

Brian looked around at the debris and picked his way across to the back door, where he unwedged the wooden chair from the door handle. The door swung open slightly in the wind, scraping to a stop on a carpet of broken glass.

George nodded towards his desired location for it. He waited for Brian to sit, then crossed the kitchen, stumbling slightly before steadying himself against the counter. He was careful not to turn his back on his guest. Making sure that Brian could see, George lifted a large bread knife from its wooden holder on the worktop. He released the lever on the shotgun and the barrel swung down over his arm. He nodded to Brian, emphasising the gesture of trust, then awkwardly extracted the two cartridges and put them in one of the droopy pockets of his cardigan.

"Thank you, George," said Brian. "Guns make me nervous."

George smiled and placed the shotgun on the counter, then held the knife by his side, making no attempt to hide it. Brian followed it with his eyes.

"Just in case Brian," said George.

Brian gave an uneasy smile.

"Do you have a first aid kit, George?"

"Yes, but there's not much in it."

"Let's have a look," said Brian.

George opened a long cupboard in the corner and retrieved the first aid box, nearly dropping the knife in the process. He handed the small tin box to Brian.

"Okay," said Brian as he flicked through the contents of the very basic medical kit. "Let's see what we're dealing with, shall we?"

He rose slowly and gestured for George to take the chair.

George lowered himself onto the chair, fighting back the usual noises and grunts that his well-worn body made. He held the knife on his lap and grimaced when a tug on the masking tape, holding his makeshift dressing in place, sent a stab of pain through his head. Brian unwrapped the bandage and gauge and furrowed his brow when he saw the wound.

"That's a fairly nasty laceration, George. You'd really need stitches," said Brian. "I'm guessing you don't have a suture kit?"

George shook his head slowly, feeling the pain more now that his wound was exposed to the air.

"Okay," said Brian, searching the room, and his memory, for a solution. "Do you have any super glue?"

George squinted at him. "Super glue? Just normal super glue?"

"Yes, it's perfectly safe, the military would use it in the field," said Brian. "When the power comes back on you can get it seen to properly in the hospital."

"If the power comes back on," said George. He pointed to a drawer beside the sink. "There should be some in there, but it might be all dried up."

Brian found the glue and checked that it was still usable. He filled a bowl with water from the still warm kettle and used a towel to clean George's wound.

"So, what caused this?" asked Brian as he wiped the area with an antiseptic wipe from the medical kit.

"I got hit on the head with the butt of that," said George, directing his eyes to the shotgun.

"And you still managed to stop all three of them?"

George shifted in his seat, suddenly uncomfortable with recanting the events.

"It wasn't just me, there were others here too."

"Others?" asked Brian with an inquisitive tilt of the head, focus still on George's wound.

"Yeah, a wee girl crashed her car into the gate and I brought her in here. When she came round, she was frantic, saying that escaped prisoners were after her, and sure enough, they turned up a couple of hours later."

"Right?" said Brian. "Okay, I'm going to put this glue on now. It might sting a little."

George nodded gingerly.

"You'll need to keep your eyes closed, though. The fumes from this stuff can really irritate them."

George looked up at Brian for a moment, then closed his eyes. The sweet scent of the adhesive was already making him dizzy.

"So, tell me about your wife, George," said Brian as he finished securing the new bandage on George's head. "What's her condition?"

CHAPTER 6

Brian sat on the stool beside Rose's bed, his head tilted as he starred in silence at her sleeping form, the duvet and blanket gently rising and falling with each shallow breath. He thought his days of tending to patients were long gone, his years of training and experience were no longer of use. His attention finally turned to the myriad of medications crowding the bedside table. There were bottles and blister packs of pills, liquid medicines, and ointments. He checked the labels and the dosage instructions, and took notice of the small quantities that were left as he shook the bottles in turn.

"So, you haven't been able to get your latest prescription filled?" asked Brian.

"No, not since the power went out. We were supposed to get them on Monday, so that's nearly a week," said George, who then frowned deeply. "This's Sunday, right?"

"Saturday," said Brian without looking up.

"Right, Saturday. I usually only stay a week ahead," said George, who stood by the door looking anxious. He was holding the shotgun again, but Brian wasn't sure if he'd reloaded it.

Brian bobbed his head. "You've only a couple of days' worth left. But I'm sure you know that," he said, turning to George with a sympathetic smile.

"Yeah," said George. "I know."

Brian stood. "Okay, let's have a look at the patient."

Reaching forward, he placed the back of his hand gently on Rose's forehead. Without a stethoscope or even a thermometer, there wasn't much he could do by way of an examination, certainly not while she was sleeping.

"How has she been recently?" he asked as he finished taking her pulse.

"She's been sleeping most of the time, really," said George.

Brian pursed his lips and nodded. "I think that's to be expected." He turned back to Rose and leaned in, placing his ear close to her face to listen to her breathing.

"But she was awake this morning for about an hour. She was in great form," said George, the hope in his voice evident. "Do you think she could be on the mend?"

Terminal Lucidity, thought Brian. He'd seen it countless times before. *I really have come just in time.* Rotating fully on the stool he rested his elbows on his knees and stared down at his interlinked hands before slowly raising his gaze, "I'm sorry George, but from what you've told me, I really don't think that'll be the case.

It was more likely a surge or Terminal Lucidity. Have you heard the term?"

George's shoulders slumped as he looked forlornly down at his wife. He nodded slowly. He'd heard the term, and deep down he probably suspected as much, but he'd kept that thought locked away and replaced it with hope.

"She just seemed so full of life earlier," said George. "That's the most alert she's been in weeks."

Brian nodded with a smile. "Well, I can check on her again when she wakes and we'll take it from there."

"Yes, that'd be great. You'll see. She seems to be doing much better."

Brian stood and looked to the door, waiting for George to give him direction, or permission.

"You're probably still hungry, are you?" asked George.

"Yes," said Brian enthusiastically.

"A cheese sandwich is the best I can offer, I'm afraid," said George, gesturing for Brian to lead the way downstairs.

George's feet were heavy as he negotiated the stairs again. Going down was harder than going up as the big shotgun got in the way of the handrail and blocked his view of the steps. He followed Brian through into the kitchen and motioned for him to sit. He was a little more comfortable with the doctor, but his escaped convict status kept George from trusting him fully.

Angled awkwardly, so as not to have his back turned fully to Brian, George filled the kettle and placed it on the stove. He was thankful that his delivery of bottled gas had arrived just before the power cut. He now had whatever was left in the current bottle and another full one. That'd likely last him for a few weeks. *Food will be the issue long before that*, he thought, as he took the remains of a batch loaf from the bread bin. There were about seven or eight slices left.

"The bread's a bit stale," he said, turning to Brian, still not allowing himself to be as cordial as he'd be to a normal visitor, but no longer displaying outright hostility.

"Ah, don't worry about it," said Brian with a laugh. "I'd eat your shoe if you put a bit of cheese on it."

"Ha, well, it's not that bad. It'll be fine with a cup of tea," said George with a smile.

A strained silence followed as George stared at the kettle and, from the corner of his eye, at Brian, who was surveying the broken and ransacked kitchen. George had tended to the bare minimum when Lisa and the others had left the day before. He'd wedged the back door closed, replaced some drawers that'd been ripped out, and kicked the remnants of the other kitchen chair into the corner. That had been Rose's chair. Other than that, he'd only cleared a small bit of the worktop, on which he now had a tray with two cups and two small sandwich plates.

"Would you mind carrying that please?" George asked Brian, who was staring intently at the dry stale-breaded cheese sandwich. Lifting the shotgun from where he'd it propped against the counter, George stepped back to let Brian lift the tray.

Brian's eyes left the sandwich for a moment to acknowledge, with a nod and a half smile, that George was now carrying the shotgun down by his side by the barrel. Another concession. *Don't make me regret it*, thought George.

In the living room, George sat on the left-hand seat of a three-seater settee which faced the front window. Before yesterday, he could count on one hand the number of times he'd sat in that spot. His chair was diagonally opposite, facing the TV. But this settee had been his sentry post for most of the night as he watched for more escapee visitors.

Brian now sat in George's seat, where he was politely devouring the meagre sandwich. George nibbled on his own sandwich. He was too tired to eat. Taking a sip of his tea, he closed his eyes as the soothing steam rose up around them. He couldn't allow himself to sleep while this stranger was in his house, but then again, he couldn't sleep even if he sent him on his way.

"You look like you could do with some sleep, George," said Brian when he'd finished his sandwich. "I assume you've been up all night?"

"Yeah, I had to keep an eye out for more of your friends," said George. He adjusted the shotgun which lay across his lap, nearly spilling his cup as he did so.

"They aren't my friends. I'll tell you that," said Brian defensively.

George grunted, took another mouthful of tea, and finished the last bit of the first half of his sandwich. He could see Brian eyeing the other half enviously.

"Do you want that?" asked George, gesturing to the plate. "I'm not hungry."

"Are you sure?"

"Yeah." George held out the small plate, his hand trembling with fatigue.

Brian rose from the chair and approached slowly, the tension between the two still palpable.

"Thank you, George," said Brian, taking the sandwich and retreating to his chair.

Silence returned while Brian finished off the rest of George's sandwich, which didn't take him long.

Movement outside caught George's eye, and he sat forward with a groan. Brian turned to see what George was focusing on. Two figures stood at the bottom of the garden. They were examining Lisa's car. One of them ducked inside through the broken driver's side window. George pushed himself to his feet and hefted the shotgun. He hadn't reloaded it since Brian had re-bandaged his head.

Splitting his attention between the men outside and the job of reloading the gun, George fumbled with the release switch. He reached into his cardigan pocket and immediately regretted having put the shells there. They were now jumbled with his reading glasses, a handkerchief, and a few other bits and pieces that always seemed to live in his pockets. His fingers finally gained purchase on one of the shells, which he pulled out along with his glasses, which fell to the floor with a crack. He approached the window, blew on the shell to free it from the pocket fluff that'd clung to it, and slotted it into the shotgun.

Having found nothing of interest in the car — George having retrieved everything of value from it after he'd found Lisa — the two men seemed to be in debate as to their next move. They looked towards the house. George slotted the second shell into the gun and snapped it closed, then turned towards the front door to ensure that they made the right decision.

"I think they're leaving," said Brian, who was perched on the end of his chair watching the men.

George returned to the window and was relieved to see the two men continuing their trek along the road and away from his house.

With the latest burst of adrenaline now ebbing from him, George slumped onto the settee once more.

CHAPTER 7

Brian strained his neck to see the last glimpse of Dermot and Thomas as they faded around a bend. He was glad they'd decided not to approach the house; he guessed George wouldn't have been as understanding had the two younger men knocked on his door.

Looking over at George, Brian could see that the events of the day before were catching up on the pensioner. He was slouched in the seat, his head bowed, as he absently stroked the shotgun which lay across his lap.

"I take it the phones aren't working then, George?" asked Brian, seeing the wall phone sitting on the table beside George, its long lead snaking back through to the kitchen.

"Huh?" said George groggily. "Oh, the phone. Yes, it is working, but I can't get through to anyone."

Brian finished his tea and leaned back into the chair. He was tired, having had little sleep himself over the previous few nights.

"You said there were others here yesterday," said Brian. "Where'd they go?"

"Yeah, they were friends of the girl who crashed her car. They recognised it as they were passing," said George with a sigh. "It's a good thing they stopped, or we'd be the ones lying in the garden."

"That was lucky."

"One of them was a guard from the prison," said George.

Brian frowned. "What?"

"Yeah, David Henry. No, Derek Henry or something," said George, shaking his head. "Ah, I can't remember..."

"Derek Henderson?" interrupted Brian. "Was his name, Derek Henderson?"

"Yeah, that's it, Derek."

Brian couldn't believe that the man who'd locked them in their cages and abandoned them, had been here just the day before.

"So, he killed them?" asked Brian, nodding towards the garden.

George paused for a moment before answering. "He saved us. If he and the other guy hadn't turned up when they did…"

Brian could see that George wasn't keen on talking about it, so he changed the subject, "Looks like you and Rose did a fair bit of travelling," he said, looking at the many photos positioned on the mantle and around the room.

George smiled, reminiscing. "Yeah, we did a cruise most years." He let out another deep sigh.

"Listen George, you need to sleep," said Brian. "You can trust me. I'll stay right here and if anyone comes or if I hear Rose, I'll wake you."

George didn't reply. But he didn't seem to have much choice. He was having trouble keeping his head up.

Brian turned his gaze to the window. Outside, the dark clouds were finally starting to leak. Fat, heavy raindrops began to patter on the glass, slowly to start, then intensifying as the sky darkened further. He turned to comment on it, but George had already succumbed to the exhaustion, deflating in his seat, his shoulders sagging and his chin resting on a nest of grey beard. He still cradled the huge shotgun.

Brian sat quietly, unmoving, and studied his host. George seemed like a decent man who'd had a long and happy life. Looking around the room, he could see the memories from the couple's many adventures — photos and ornaments and travel books. *I should just go,* he thought. He looked out at the rain — cold and steady — then to George, who softly purred into his cushion of hair. George had brought him in, fed him, trusted him. *But they need my help*, thought Brian.

George fidgeted and lifted his head, then mumbled and settled. Brian watched silently, consciously still. A smile spread up through his face, a compassionate, affectionate smile. *I will help them*, he thought.

###

Brian gently lifted an errant strand of grey-white hair which lay across Rose's face and tucked it neatly behind her ear. He admired her innocence, her vulnerability.

Rose reminded Brian of his own grandmother. Although his image of his granny was built mainly from the photographs that hung in his mother's house — he'd been only eight years old when she'd passed. But Rose, lying peacefully, reminded him of her as she was when he'd last seen her on the day she died. He'd been sitting on a hard plastic chair beside her bed in the sitting room of his childhood home, which had been converted into a bedroom for his grandmother, who was *not too well*, according to Brian's mother.

Every day, for the two weeks that his granny had been staying with them, Brian would come in from school and sit by her bed. With his legs swinging gently and his toes barely scraping the floor, Brian would study his granny as she slept — he hadn't seen her awake since they'd brought her home. Every day, he'd find something new to focus on — the forest of medicine boxes jostling for position on the small bedside table, the plastic tube that snaked across the room from a large oxygen tank and rested just below her nose, and the bag of clear liquid that hung from a metal stand above her bed and slowly dripped into another tube which ended at a bandage on the back of her hand. From what he'd overheard, all of these things were needed to keep her alive. Some days, he'd just stand and watch as she slept, wondering if she'd ever wake. Brian remembered how, when his grandfather had died the year before, everyone would say that he'd gone to a better place. He wondered when his granny would go to this *better place*.

It was a Friday — he remembered because his mum always made smelly fish on a Friday and he could smell it wafting through from the kitchen. That was the day that Brian had helped his granny get to the *better place*, or so he liked to think. He wanted to do something nice for her, so he manoeuvred the leg of the chair and positioned it on top of the oxygen tube then, reaching across the bedside table on his tiptoes, he twisted the small lever at the bottom of the bag of liquid to make it drip faster. He sat back on the chair and waited. Watching her intently, he wondered if he'd see the moment when she left. But nothing happened. It wasn't until after dinner, when he heard his mother cry out, that he realised that she'd gone. And he'd missed it.

Brian gazed down at Rose, a sympathetic smile curling his pursed lips. Fate had brought him here — the power cut, the guards withdrawing, him turning left instead of right — all so that he could help George and Rose.

Brian gripped the pillow tightly at either side. He looked down at Rose one last time. "You go on now, Rose, go to a better place," he whispered. He pressed down hard and felt Rose jerk into a weak resistance, her frail body suddenly fighting for life. Brian added his bodyweight to the press and waited. The struggle from Rose, for all that it had been, stopped.

Brian stood back. For a moment, his smile was gone. He looked on in awe, his eyes wide and his mouth open in anticipation. Then the smile returned.

A noise from the floor below wrenched him from his euphoric trance. He snapped back to the room. George was awake. He tossed the pillow on the bed and quickly straightened Rose's head, then ran to the top of the stairs.

"George, George, you need to come quickly," shouted Brian.

CHAPTER 8

George looked up, the doctor's words sending a chill through him. Necessity spurred him on as he clutched at the handrail and used the shotgun like a hiker's pole. He paused at the top and met Brian's eyes as he stepped back to let George through.

"I'm sorry, George," said Brian, bowing his head.

"Ah no, ah no, Rose," George's words fell heavy as he stumbled towards his wife's bed. He discarded the shotgun, which rested momentarily against the bed, then clattered unnoticed to the floor. George sat on the edge of the bed, his hands cupped around his mouth. A blink sent a cascade of tears down his face. *It wasn't supposed to be like this,*

Rose, he thought. *We had more photos to look at.*

"You didn't even see my shirt," he whispered, his mouth given permission for the briefest of smiles.

"I'm so sorry, George," said Brian, who had now moved to the foot of the bed.

George looked at him through wet eyes. "What happened? Why didn't you wake me?"

"I heard her cough, and I came up, and... I'm sorry, George, she was already gone."

George's head dropped, and he looked back at his wife. He brushed the hair back from her face. "Ah, love," he said as he stretched over and kissed her on the forehead. His eyes fell on a small trickle of blood that ran from her nose on to her upper lip. He straightened again and sighed. As he fussed with the quilt and tidied it in around her, he lifted an out-of-place pillow to return it to where it belonged. He paused in confusion, the creases on his wrinkled forehead deepening. A spot of blood, fresh and smeared, marked the centre of the pristine white pillowcase. He stared at it for a moment, then back to Rose's nose.

He turned to Brian, a question not yet fully formed. Brian looked at the pillow in George's hands, and then at George, and then at the shotgun lying by George's feet. Before George could verbalise his confusion, the stark realisation hit him. A tsunami of emotions washed away his sadness and grief, leaving only hate, vengeance, murder. George followed Brian's eyes to the shotgun. Brian clearly registered the sudden epiphany on George's face. He weighed up his options while already backing towards the door, then turned and bolted for the stairs.

George moved faster than he had done in thirty years. He snatched up the shotgun, fumbling it into position as he moved to the door. As fast as his reactions seemed, they were too slow to catch the younger man. Brian was already on the bottom stair and reaching for the door. George swung the long barrel of the shotgun over the banister and with hope and rage, he pulled both triggers at once. The double recoil of the massive gun sent George staggering backwards. The two shots had torn through the handrail at the bottom of the stairs and left the front door frame a mess of broken timber and plaster. He couldn't see if he'd hit his target.

As George picked his way through the debris on the lower stairs, he heard it, a moaning cry of agony. He stepped through the remains of his front door and saw Brian on all fours in a desperate scramble for escape. He dragged his right leg behind him, his calf a ragged mess of torn muscle and flesh. The trail of blood was already being washed away by the now torrential rain.

As George approached, Brian sensed his presence and flopped on to his back, still trying feebly to drag himself backwards on his elbows. The heavy rain pasted his mud-covered shirt to his heaving chest. One of his shoes had been kicked off and lay in his wake, blood soaked and scuffed. He looked up at George, his face twisted in agony, his eyes pleading for mercy.

"It was the right thing to do, George," said Brian, panting through the pain.

George glared down at his wife's murderer.

"It wasn't right to let her suffer, George. I'm a doctor, George. I had to help her."

Brian continued to edge backwards, crawling on his elbows and pushing himself along with his good foot.

George followed slowly. He didn't speak, his face gnarled by the burning emotions surging through him. His tears of anguish and hatred were instantly diluted by stinging sheets of rain.

"Your wife was in pain, George," Brian coughed and spluttered and tried to back away further. "I helped her."

George stepped closer and placed his boot on Brian's ruined calf. A wail of pain erupted from the doctor and his retreat ceased. George pressed his weight down on the raw wound.

"Are you in pain, Brian?" growled George. "Do you want me to help you?"

"No, no George, I was doing a good thing."

George reached into his cardigan pocket and withdrew his last two cartridges. Slowly, he reloaded the shotgun, ignoring the squirms and screams and pleads from Brian.

The two men locked eyes. George pointed the gun at the cowering doctor, who screamed in agony and terror. An animal like roar erupted from the old man's throat and he pulled the trigger.

Countless birds abandoned the shelter of the nearby trees and took to the hostile skies. George turned and slowly trundled back to the doorway. Four men now lay dead in his garden.

CHAPTER 9

George held his wife's hand, his face buried in the soft duvet. He didn't know how long he'd sat there. Time had no meaning. The rain had stopped and a blade of sun had cut through the thinning clouds. He could feel the heat on his back as it angled through the bedroom window. The rest of him was wet and cold, the cardigan now heavy and stretched.

With a groan of fatigue, he pushed himself up from the bed and shuffled through to the bathroom. He discarded the wet clothes and the sodden bandage from his head. The glued wound sat ugly and proud, but was no longer bleeding. He washed his face, brushed his hair and his thick beard, and dressed in another of the Hawaiian shirts that Rose loved so much.

Returning to her side, he propped himself up beside her and continued where they'd left off in the well-thumbed photo album. He paused at each photo, conjuring the memories of their many adventures. He could feel his head beginning to lighten. Smiling through the tears, he closed the album, resting his hand on the cover affectionately.

George placed the album on the stool and reached behind the now-empty pill bottles to retrieve his favourite photo. His numbing fingers struggled for purchase on the silver frame. With a shaking hand, he balanced the photo on his chest and chuckled at the scene.

"I always told you I'd follow you anywhere, my love."

He leaned down and kissed his wife on the forehead. Through the window, he saw the clearing sky and the green hills stretching into the distance. With a contented sigh, he smiled and closed his heavy eyes.

The End

Reviews

I hope you enjoyed Dr Death, if you did, please consider leaving a short review. Links to the various sites can be found here
https://linktr.ee/pmcmurrough

No matter how short, reviews are very important for independent authors.
Thank you, I look forward to reading your review.

www.ingramcontent.com/pod-product-compliance
Lightning Source LLC
Chambersburg PA
CBHW030823200726
48288CB00004B/1365